THE REVENGE OF THE

GREEN PLANET

THE EDEN PROJECT BOOK OF
ASTOUNDING !
FACTS ABOUT PLANTS ◆

THE REVENGE OF THE GREEN PLANET
ASTOUNDING FACTS ABOUT PLANTS
AN EDEN PROJECT BOOK 1903 919053

Published in Great Britain in 2002 by Eden Project Books,
an imprint of Transworld Publishers

1 3 5 7 9 10 8 6 4 2

Eden Project Books are published by
Transworld Publishers,
61-63 Uxbridge Road, London W5 5SA,
a division of The Random House Group Ltd,
in Australia by Random House Australia (Pty) Ltd,
20 Alfred Street, Milsons Point, Sydney, NSW 2061,
Australia,
in New Zealand by Random House New Zealand Ltd,
18 Poland Road, Glenfield, Auckland 10, New Zealand,
and in South Africa by Random House (Pty) Ltd,
Endulini, 5A Jubilee Road, Parktown 2193, South Africa

Printed and bound in Great Britain by
Clays Ltd, St Ives plc.

www.booksattransworld.co.uk

www.edenproject.com

With special thanks to Dr Jo Readman
at the Eden Project.

CONTENTS

THE REVENGE OF THE
GREEN PLANET

It's time to sit up and take notice of the living green things around you. Plants are the dominant life-form on Earth, making up around 99% of the biomass (the total number of living things), so perhaps it's also time to start showing a bit of respect ... and understanding.

If you could shrink to the size of an insect and speed up the world around you, you'd see just how plants move and communicate, reproduce and grow. Because of course, plants do all these things, but so slowly that most of us don't really notice.

Sadly, shrinking and fast-forwarding aren't possible in real life, but this book is the next best thing. And before you assume that we're only talking about the green things in the garden and the countryside, look around the room you're in at all the things that have come from plants. Paper, if you're still in the bookshop. Food and drink, if you're in the kitchen. Wooden furniture in the living room. Scented soap and medicines in the bathroom. Cotton sheets and pillowcases in the bedroom. Clothes ... musical instruments ... cricket bats – the list is endless. Plants are everywhere, indoors and out.

Enjoy finding out more!

The Eden Project in Cornwall is dedicated to bringing people and plants together. The facts in this book have been gathered from many different sources by the people who work there. Sometimes plant facts are difficult to verify, however, so we will welcome any corrections or additions for a future edition.

QUIZ

HOW MANY PLANTS HAVE YOU USED TODAY?

You probably use far more plants in a day than you think. Try this quiz to get you started. Answers at the back of the book.

(1) **FROM WHICH** tree do we get the latex that goes to make our Wellington boots and washing-up gloves?

(2) **WHICH PLANT** can be used to make tasty food and sweets, doormats, and can even end up as an ingredient in shampoo?

(3) **WHAT IS** the name of the snack, made from *Zea mays*, which is often eaten at the cinema?

4 **FROM** which plant do we make both chocolate and hand cream?

5 **WHICH** plant are sheets and pillowcases often made from?

6 **WHICH HERB** gets its name from the Latin 'lavare', meaning to wash?

7 **WHICH TREE** is found in churchyards, makes a good hedge, and yields a chemical called taxol, which is being trialled as a possible treatment for cancer?

8 **NOW USED** as a hair dye and a brown tattoo, this plant once provided the colour for an Egyptian mummy's bandages.

9 **YOU'VE** almost certainly used paper today. What sort of plant is it usually made from?

10 **DELICIOUS** in a fruit salad, and with ham on a pizza, this fruit contains a medicine that may help thrombosis sufferers.

11 **NAME** a plant that often grows in water, is eaten by millions of people every day and makes our breakfast cereal rather noisy!

8

(12) **WHICH PALM** gives us ingredients for soap, margarine, candles and a type of fuel?

(13) **PLANTS** photosynthesize. They take in water and carbon dioxide and, using the sun's energy, turn it into sugar and a gas that we are very grateful for. What is this gas called?

(14) **THE LEAVES** of this plant are used to make a favourite hot (or sometimes iced) drink.

Now you have discovered some of the ways in which people use plants, how many do you think you have used today?

9

OFF YOUR TROLLEY

Many items in your supermarket trolley come from plants – and not just food!

TEA AND COFFEE

PEOPLE in the western world have been taking tea breaks for over two hundred years.

MANILA HEMP, which is the material used to make most tea bags, comes from a close relation of the banana.

IN TIBET people sometimes mix tea with yak's milk, butter, salt and spice to make a nourishing tea soup, a valuable addition to their diet.

BLACK TEA should be made with boiling water. As the boiling water hits the leaves they uncurl, known in the trade as the 'agony of the leaves'.

THE CHINESE were using tea as a medicine thousands of years before we used it as a hot drink.

IN JAPANESE LEGEND, a Buddhist monk was said to have cut off his eyelids to prevent himself falling asleep during a seven-year contemplation of Buddha. Where his eyelids fell, the first tea plants grew, to help others stay awake without resorting to such extremes.

CENTURIES AGO the Chinese pressed tea dust into bricks and used them to trade with their Russian neighbours. Russian people crumbled chunks of the tea bricks into their samovars (elaborate traditional tea urns) to make a brew.

TEA TIME!

TEA easily picks up flavours, and so cannot be stored near other smelly plants (e.g. bananas). You can put used teabags in the fridge to get rid of strong smells.

EXPERIENCED tea-pickers can each collect up to 35 kg of tea leaves a day, about the same weight as an average ten-year-old child. This gives 9 kg of processed black tea, equivalent to 72 packets of tea.

RICH PICKINGS!

THE TANNIN found in tea (also in roses and oak trees) is probably used by the plant to deter insects.

COFFEE BEANS grow inside coffee 'cherries', which ripen all year round on coffee bushes. The cherries are picked, usually by hand, when they are red and ripe ...

BEANS

RED & SHINY

PALE GREEN & STICKY

...Two beans are extracted from each cherry. The beans are green and do not turn brown or smell of coffee until they are roasted.

THE FIRST coffee-drinker may have been a sheikh of the Sufi order who started to roast, grind and brew coffee beans round about the beginning of the fifteenth century in the port of Mocha.

COFFEE is one of the leading internationally traded commodities in the world.

COFFEE originated in Africa, but it is now also grown in Asia and Latin America.

COFFEE HOUSES reached Britain in 1637 and soon became known as 'penny universities', the places to go to get the latest news and views.

CEREALS

DID YOU eat grass for breakfast today? If you have eaten Rice Krispies, Corn Flakes, Shredded Wheat or toast (made from wheat flour) the answer is yes. They are all made from types of grasses.

FOR THE SWEET TOOTH

COCOA PODS grow from the trunk of the tree. The beans inside the pod are put in the sun to ferment, which brings out the scent and flavour of the chocolate.

THE BOTANICAL name for cocoa, *Theobroma cacao* means food (broma) of the gods (theos).

MANY CHILDREN of cocoa farmers around the world have never tasted chocolate. Many chocolate-eating children have never seen a cocoa pod.

WOMEN eat far more chocolate than men. Children eat nearly as much ...

THE SUGAR you put in your tea or on your cereal usually comes from sugar cane or sugar beet.

THE SUGAR in some drinks is made from corn syrup.

NATURAL chewing gum comes from trees! Chicle is a milky fluid inside the sapodilla tree (*Manilkara zapota*) that grows in tropical forests.

SOMETHING TO CHEW ON

THE TASTE of your cola drink originally came from the African rainforests too! It was made from the nuts of the *Cola nitida* tree.

THE INGREDIENTS of Coca-Cola are a well-kept secret. We think we may know some of the ingredients:

sugar, from sugar cane or sugar beet.

caramel, made of burnt sugar.

caffeine, a chemical found in the cola tree, coffee and tea.

phosphoric acid.

cola nut extract.

citric acid.

sodium citrate.

Most of these are common plant-based ingredients, but the real taste and mystery still reside in a secret recipe that no one is allowed to find out.

TOP SECRET!

16

BOOZE

AT THE BEGINNING
of the twenty-first century 1%
of the world's population worked
growing, making or selling wine.

WITHOUT THE MARRIAGE
between the bark of the cork
oak tree and a bottle tall enough
to lie on its side, fine matured
wine could never have been
discovered. Oxygen 'breathes'
very slowly through the damp cork
and allows the wine to mature.

CORK OAKS, unlike most trees,
regrow their bark. This can be
stripped off at around nine to
twelve year intervals for up to
two hundred years.

THE CORK TREE has its first
strip for cork at around twenty-
five years old.

AN AVERAGE cork tree can
cork four thousand bottles.

DO the wine-drinkers in your family buy wine bottled with real corks, rather than plastic ones? If so, they will be supporting cork farmers and also helping to save the forty-two species of birds, including the rare and endangered Black vulture and the snake-eating Short-toed eagle, which nest in cork trees.

THE WORLD'S largest cork tree – the Whistler tree – grows in the Alentejo region of Portugal and will be 220 years old in 2003. It is named after the many songbirds that live in its branches. Each harvest produces enough cork for 100,000 wine bottles.

COOKING INGREDIENTS

VEGETABLE OILS can be made from sunflowers, palm trees, soybeans, oil seed rape, peanuts, olives and even cotton.

SUNFLOWER OIL, which we use to fry food and spread on our bread in margarine, is also a component of some racing car engine oils.

GREASED LIGHTNING!

MUSTARD contains chemical glycosides and an enzyme, myrosin. In the plant these are kept apart from each other and are quite safe. However, when the seed is chomped or ground up with water ... zap! The enzyme reacts with the glycosides and the fiery hot mustard oil (or isothiocyanate if you prefer) is released.

READ the packet and you'll find that lots of foods, such as yoghurts and sauces, contain thickeners made from plants.

agar, from seaweed

carrageenan, from a seaweed known as Irish moss

cornflour, from maize

guar, from an Indian bean

gum Arabic, from a tree called *Acacia senegal*

locust bean gum

YOU OFTEN find colourings listed on the food packet too.

annatto, a red dye from a tropical tree called *Bixa orellana*

anthocyanin, a red plant dye

B carotene, the orange colouring from carrots

caramel, from burnt sugar

chlorophyll, the green colouring in plants

20

PAINTS and clothes sometimes contain blue dye from indigo-producing plants such as woad.

TOILETRIES

SOME LIPSTICKS may contain extracts from coconut oil, linseed oil, soybean oil, castor oil, jojoba oil and, most importantly, carnauba wax from the leaf of the Brazilian waxpalm.

TOOTHPASTE often contains mint for flavouring. Other plant products in the tube can include: cotton (cellulose for shape); gooey extracts from wood pulp (to make the gel flow); a sugar alcohol made from wheat and maize starch (to stop it drying out); seaweed (a thickener); and coconut and palm oil (as foaming agents).

SEAWEED
COTTON
COCONUT
WOOD
MAIZE

LOOFAHS are skeletons of the marrow-like Luffa fruit.

MOST AFTER-SUN lotions contain sap from the Aloe vera plant, which is very soothing. If you have an *Aloe vera* plant you can cut off a small piece and use the sap directly on sunburnt skin to cool it down.

COMMON PLANTS used in making perfumes include roses, lavender, jasmine, rosemary and geranium. Some perfumes contain over a hundred carefully blended ingredients.

JOJOBA OIL, used in shampoo, can also be used as engine oil.

MOST SOAP used to be made with animal fat, but today more and more plant oils are being used, including those extracted from coconut palms, African oil palms and olives.

DAISY FRESH

CASTOR OIL, once used just as a medicine, is now also used in bath oil. Other plant oils are added for relaxation and scent, such as lavender, geranium and bergamot.

COCOA BUTTER is a useful ingredient in moisturizers and face creams because it melts at skin temperature.

HAND CREAM

FABRICS

COTTON FABRIC is made from the hairs on the seeds. Each hair is three thousand times as long as it is wide.

IF BRITAIN grew all the cotton it used, the cotton crops would take up roughly a fifth of its farmland.

COTTON is the world's biggest non-food crop, and makes half the world's textiles. In developing countries, most cotton is grown by smallholders and not exported. China is the biggest producer, followed by the USA, which produces 70% of all exported cotton.

GREAT THREADS!

COTTON CROPS take up over thirty-three million hectares worldwide, an area bigger than the British Isles.

COTTON is a natural fibre as opposed to one produced from chemicals, but cotton growers spray vast quantities of chemicals on the plants in the form of pesticides, so it's not quite so 'natural' after all!

WOOL, from sheep, is only one stage removed from plants, as without grass there would be no sheep!

SILK is made from the cocoons of silkworms. Silkworms feed on a special diet of mulberry leaves and could not exist without them.

LINEN is woven from the fibres in the stems of the pretty flower called blue flax. Linen, still fashionable today, was being worn ten thousand years ago. The Romans wore it, the Greeks wore it and the Egyptians wrapped their dead in it!

HEMP is possibly the oldest plant-based fabric, but it is also one of the most modern and most versatile. Today hemp is used in clothing, carpeting, sails, draperies and industrial clothing and has the advantages of being hard-wearing, recyclable, and resistant to both fire and sunlight.

KIDS

BIG SOFTY

THE SOFT padding in most disposable nappies comes from wood pulp.

KAPOK stuffing for cushions and soft toys comes from the seeds of the kapok tree. The fibres are airtight and watertight, making them warm and buoyant.

STATIONERY

WHAT IS paper made of?

58% wood pulp - Nearly all paper is made from wood, but only a few types of tree are used. One third of the world's harvest of smaller trees is used to make paper.

38% waste paper - Our cities and offices (the urban forest) supply raw material for recycled paper.

4% non-wood pulp - Waste from plant crops (as well as plants grown specifically for their fibres) helps take the pressure off the forests. Hemp, cotton and flax are used to make bank notes. Seven to eight million tonnes of bamboo are pulped each year to make paper.

ONE TREE per person is felled every year in the US to produce newspapers and magazines.

THE CHINESE were using paper more or less as we know it around AD 100. It was made from bark, hemp and rags.

THE FIRST paper mill in Britain, built in 1488, used old clothes and rags as raw material. Early mills were not very successful because people thought that the discarded rags helped to spread the Plague.

WHAT CONNECTS the Ancient Britons and computer technology? They both use woad; one as a dye for body painting, the other as a printing ink.

WOAD

INK

WASPS might have been the inspiration behind making paper from wood. Wasps make their nests from a sort of cardboard produced by chewing wood and mixing it with saliva.

MOST of the wood and paper imported into the UK comes from the northern forests of the world in places like Scandinavia and Canada.

HOW TO SAVE PAPER!

REDUCE Use less paper and packaging.

REUSE Write on the back; use it again for something else; compost it.

RECYCLE Recycle your paper and use recycled paper.

REGENERATE Use paper from sustainable forests.

A TRIP ROUND THE DEPARTMENT STORE

Plants for painting, plants for play, plants for music ...

HOBBIES

OIL PAINTS contain linseed oil from flax seeds. Some oil paints use poppy seed oil and sunflower seed oil.

TURPENTINE, the oil paint thinner, is traditionally made from pine trees.

SPORT

ASH is Britain's toughest timber. It has strong and flexible wood which can absorb shocks without splintering.

30

MANY YEARS AGO the Anglo-Saxons used ash to make handles and spears. More recently ash became the wood for sport - it was used for tennis racquets, hockey sticks, baseball bats and oars. Oars are still made from ash but the others are now more often made from fibreglass, carbon fibre and other composite materials.

A CRICKET BAT is made from many plants. The bat itself is crafted from the willow tree, *Salix alba* var. *caerulea*. It is treated with linseed oil (made from the seeds of the flax plant). The handle is made from strips of rattan (a climbing plant from the tropics), sandwiched with rubber (the latex from a tropical tree).

B.A.T.

THE WOOD *Guaiacum officinale* (from Lignum vitae, the tree of life), which is used to make bowling balls, is one of the heaviest woods in the world.

BILLIARD CUES often have butts made from rosewood or ebony, and shafts of ash or maple.

HOW DO YOU get golf balls to spin faster in the air? Well, professional golfers often use balls covered in balata rather than plastic. Balata is a type of rubber tapped from trees in South America.

MUSICAL INSTRUMENTS

TREES from all over the world are used to make musical instruments. Sitka spruce from western North America is valued for soundboards on pianos, guitars and stringed instruments. The trees need to be two to three hundred years old for the best sound.

THE BACK of a violin is usually made from maple or sycamore, but for centuries the body was made from European or sitka spruce, rosewood or ebony. Now rosewoods (from Central America, Africa, India and Southeast Asia) and ebony (from the tropics of the Americas, Africa and Asia) are on the endangered list, but they are still used for pegs and tailpieces.

COOL SOUNDS!

CLARINETS and oboes are usually made from African blackwood, known as Mpingo. Mpingo trees grow in central and southern Africa, chiefly Tanzania and Mozambique.

THE DRUMS in a drum kit are usually made from maple, ash, beech or cherry, and sometimes mahogany.

FURNITURE AND FLOOR COVERINGS

WILLOW branches can be woven into 'wicker' chairs and baskets.

RATTAN makes good furniture. It comes from a climbing plant which can grow over 100m long. Luckily, the spikes on this palm are carefully removed before the furniture is made.

LINSEED OIL and real lino flooring are made from the oily seeds of flax.

RUSH MATS and chair seats are often made from bulrushes.

DOORMATS are usually made from the outer hairy fibres of the coconut.

AND THE MONEY TO PAY FOR IT ALL ...

BANK NOTES are still made from cotton, flax and hemp, sometimes after they have been made into clothes first.

RECORD BREAKERS

Imagine some of these prizewinners at the village flower show!

BIG LEAVES

THE LEAVES of the giant rhubarb plant, *Gunnera manicata*, can reach up to three metres across.

THE CLIMBING fern Lygodium has leaves up to 30 metres long.

ONE OF THE largest undivided leaves ever found was of *Alocasia macrorrhiza*, from Sabah, Malaysia. It was 3.02m long, 1.92m wide and had a surface area of 3.17 square metres.

SPEED ON STALKS

GIANT SEA KELP, the world's biggest seaweed, grows at a rate of 45cm a day in springtime.

THE LEAVES of the sensitive plant, *Mimosa pudica*, close up and turn downwards instantly when you touch them. You set off an electrical current in the leaf that empties the liquid from its base and makes it collapse. Why? Well, would you want to eat a plant that looked that sick?

THE TROPICAL giant bamboo, the fastest growing plant on the planet, was clocked growing skywards at 91cm a day.

SOME GROWERS claim to have grown sunflowers to a height of over six metres in a season.

TALLEST

TALL STORY!

THE TALLEST timber tree is the famous 'Mendocino tree', a coast redwood (*Sequoia sempervirens*) in California, USA. In December 1996, when it was one thousand years old it measured in at 112.014m. It's still growing.

THE TALIPOT palm has a flower spike seven metres high, the tallest in the plant kingdom. The spike carries up to ten million white flowers. Not surprisingly it only flowers once in its life and then dies.

GIANT SEA KELP grows 100m up from the ocean floor to reach the sunlight at the surface.

OLDEST

A FOSSIL of a flower was found in 1989, near Melbourne, Australia, which is thought to be 120 million years old.

THE OLDEST living plant is probably the King's holly (*Lomatia tasmania*) which grows in south-west Tasmania. The same plant has been growing for around forty thousand years.

ONE-HUNDRED-YEAR-OLD olive trees are mere babies compared to the bristlecone pine, which has been known to live to 5,500 years old, and the redwood in the Prairie Creek Redwoods State Park, California, USA, which is 12,000 years old.

SEEDS

THE BIGGEST seed – Coco-de-mer, or *Lodoicea maldivica* – is also known as the double coconut and grows only in the Seychelles. It's the same shape and size as a large bottom.

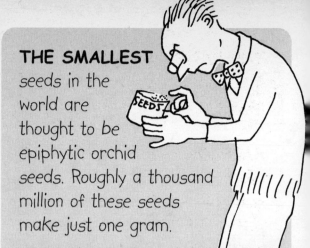

THE SMALLEST seeds in the world are thought to be epiphytic orchid seeds. Roughly a thousand million of these seeds make just one gram.

THE PRIZE for the hardiest seeds must surely go to the Arctic lupin, found in the frozen soil of northern Canada. Even though they were 10-15,000 years old, they sprouted and grew.

NOT FROZEN, but equally ancient, a Japanese magnolia tree grew from a 10,000-year-old seed!

EXPENSIVE

IT TAKES more than 80,000 of the crocus flowers, *Crocus sativus*, to produce 450g of saffron, which is used both as a spice and a yellow dye. Saffron is made from the dried red stigmas (female flowerparts).

THE WORD 'saffron' comes from the Arabic word **za'faran**, meaning yellow.

SAFFRON has always been expensive. In the Middle Ages someone caught bulking out saffron with cheaper substitutes could be burned at the stake, a punishment suffered by one Herr Findaker in 1444.

SAFFRON probably found its way into traditional Cornish cooking in the days when Cornish tin was traded with the Phoenicians.

SMELLY

WHAT'S THAT PONG?

ONE OF THE WORST smelling plants in the world is Dutchman's pipe (*Aristolochia labiata*). Its disgusting smell attracts insects to pollinate it. Its red veins and hairs make it look a little like rotting meat.

THE DURIAN fruit is said to smell of hell and taste of heaven. This spiky, football-sized fruit from the tropics is so smelly that it's not allowed on board an aircraft!

THE BIGGEST flower in the world, rafflesia, attracts flies because it smells of rotting corpses.

WHIFFY!

LONG-DISTANCE TRAVELLERS

THE SEEDS of the coconut fruit (*Cocos nucifera*) float and drift for months across the sea, washing up on shores as far away as 2,000 km from the parent tree.

GREEDY

ONE OF THE hungriest-looking plants is the pitcher plant (**Nepenthes**) from the rainforest. It's been described as a green lavatory bowl full of digesting fluid. Insects and even rats fall in, and many never get out.

PROLIFIC

EACH CATKIN on a birch tree produces between five and six million grains of pollen to ensure that some are carried on the wind to other trees.

A COMMON WEED, fat hen (*Chenopodium album*), has seventy thousand seeds per plant, leading to the saying, 'One year's weeding, seven years' seeding.'

MASSIVE

A ROSE BUSH in Arizona, USA, is so big that up to 250 people can sit under its branches. In 1998 it covered an area of 740 square metres.

ONE OF THE world's largest pumpkins ever weighed in at just over 480 kg – about the same weight as a Mini.

44

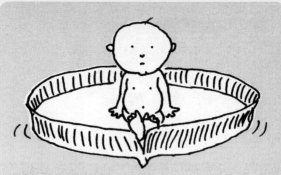

THE GIANT water lily is the world's biggest water plant. Its leaves are two metres across and strong enough to take the weight of a child. Accounts tell how women in the Amazon used to put their children on them while they worked by the river.

THE BIGGEST herbaceous plant in the world is the wild type of banana plant called *Musa ingens*. Its stem can grow up to 15 metres and its bunches of bananas can weigh up to 50 kg.

THE MOST MASSIVE tree in the world is a Giant Sequoia tree from California, USA. Called 'General Sherman', in 1998 it was 83.8 metres tall and measured 31.3 metres round the trunk.

THE BIGGEST flower is the parasite rafflesia, *Rafflesia arnoldi*, which is found in the south-east Asian jungles. With petals almost two centimetres thick, it measures nearly one metre across and weighs up to 11kg.

HARD

SOME of the hardest tissues in the vegetable kingdom are found at the base of the palm tree.

DEEP DOWN

THE DEEPEST roots belong to the wild fig tree of South Africa. They reach down an amazing 120 metres.

TOP CROPS

MAIZE is the No. 1 crop in the world, though not all of it is used for food.

RICE comes next. Rice feeds around half of the world's population.

WHEAT is number three.

POTATOES are up there with the big ones. Think of all those crisps!

GEOGRAPHICAL EXTREMES

THE MOST NORTHERLY growing plant (latitude of 83 degrees N) is thought to be the yellow poppy (*Papaver radicatum*).

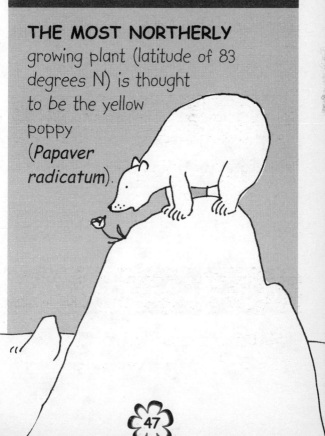

THE MOST SOUTHERLY
growing plants (latitude 86 degrees S) are possibly lichens similar to the *Rhinodina frigida*.

THE HIGHEST
plants ever found were on Mount Kamet in the Himalayas, growing at 6,400m. These were the flowering plants of *Ermania himalayensis* and *Ranunculus lobatus*.

TOP!

ALTHOUGH 99.9% of sunlight underwater is filtered out at 269m, an algae was found growing at these depths off San Salvador island, Bahamas, by marine scientists Mark and Diane Littler.

UP in the Salyut Space Station nearly twenty years ago the crew managed to grow spring onions. Cosmonaut Svetlana Savitskaya was given them with her lunch when she paid a visit!

BITES FROM HISTORY

Earth was a plant planet before it was a dinosaur planet. We came along very late in the day, but our own history also depends on our relationship with plants.

160 MILLION YEARS AGO

DINOSAURS in the Jurassic period munched on ancestors of the maidenhair tree, *Ginkgo biloba*, which is still with us today.

50 MILLION YEARS AGO

FIFTY-MILLION-YEAR-OLD palm fossils have been found in London.

10,000 YEARS AGO

ONE OF THE oldest relics of human industry is a bit of hemp fabric dating back to approximately 8,000 BC.

49

6,000 YEARS AGO	**WINE** has been made from grapes for at least six thousand years.
4,500 YEARS AGO	**THE EARLY** Egyptians were possibly using olive oil to help move the great stones they used to build the pyramids.
4,000 YEARS AGO	**WE KNOW** that peaches were being cultivated in China as long ago as 2,000BC. *WHAT A PEACH!*
2,500 YEARS AGO	**FROM THE VERY BEGINNING** of the Olympic Games the winner was crowned with an olive leaf garland crafted from the olive tree from Mount Olympia. Wearing the crown was considered a greater honour than donning gold!

THEOPHRASTUS (371-287 BC), the Greek botanist, described over 550 species of plants – including bananas. Rumour had it that he lived another 23 years and died aged 107, but 84 was still a ripe old age in those days.

IN THE 1400s Turkish law made it legal for a woman to divorce her husband if he failed to provide her with her daily quota of coffee.

WHERE'S MY COFFEE?

HENRY VIII laid down laws ensuring that farmers in his realm grew industrial hemp for making fabric.

1600s **WILLIAM HARVEY**, the great 17th century plant physiologist, thought that the plant must have a circulatory system like ours. He abandoned the idea after plant dissection failed to reveal a heart.

HEARTLESS!

1676 **IN 1676** English physician Sir Thomas Millington suggested to his colleague Nehemiah Grew that plants had sex in order to reproduce. Grew wrote a book in 1682 called *The Anatomy of Plants*, in which he said that Millington 'suggested to me that the attire (the plant stamens) doth serve as the male for the generation of the seed'.

52

1700s **IN THE EARLY DAYS** of the European coffee houses coffee was often served strong and black, sometimes boiled with eggshells, ginger, butter, mustard and other strange additives.

1721 **PHILIP MILLER** noticed in 1721 that bees were going between the flowers and for the first time it was realized that in the love affairs between plants the bees were the go-betweens, carrying the pollen from plant to plant.

1735 **THE SWEDISH NATURALIST,** Carolus Linnaeus, devised a system for classifying plants by the arrangement of the sexual parts of the flower. In his work *Philosophica Botanica*, published in 1735, he even classified other botanists according to the way they classified plants!

53

1778

LINNAEUS eventually died in a state of dementia after spending his whole working life on the classification of plants and animals. We still base some of our classification on his 'binomial' naming system, in which plant families are subdivided into genera and species.

1771– 1777

BETWEEN 1771 and 1777, the English chemist Joseph Priestley (who discovered oxygen) came to the conclusion that plants could 'repair' the air made unbreathable by animals. At first he thought that animals and plants would use up air in the same way, but he decided to check. A mouse kept under a bell jar soon died, but a sprig of green mint continued to live for days. What's more, a mouse lived when it shared the bell jar with the mint! We now know of course that oxygen is a by-product of photosynthesis.

1779

JAN INGEN-HOUSZ, a Dutchman, discovered the process of photosynthesis in 1779, when he found that plants could only produce the gas (later named as oxygen) in sunlight, and that only the green parts of plants did this.

1700s

IT WAS a Swiss minister, Senebier, who confirmed Ingen-Housz's findings – that plants could only produce oxygen if they were in sunlight – and discovered that they used carbon dioxide as a nutrient.

1800s **ONLY IN THE** 1800s did the Swiss scientist de Saussure find that plants obtained some of their nutrients from water.

1817 **CHLOROPHYLL** wasn't named until 1817, when the French chemists Pelletier and Caventou managed to isolate the green substance from plants. Chlorophyll means 'green leaf' in Greek.

1845 **IN 1845**, a German physician, Mayer, discovered that plants changed light energy into chemical energy. The term photosynthesis had been born. Scientists now realized that leaves were not flat in order to shade the plant but to act as solar panels to absorb as much sunlight as possible.

FLOWER POWER

1800s   **THOMAS EDISON** experimented with six hundred substances as filaments for his light bulb, including bamboo fibres. The first successful light bulb had a filament made from carbonized cotton.

1800s   **WHEN DARWIN** was shown the beautiful orchid *Angraecum sesquipedale* from Madagascar, he noted the foot-long tube at the back of the flower with nectar at the bottom and predicted that a moth with a tongue at least a foot long would be needed

to pollinate it. After Darwin's death, a moth was discovered in Madagascar with a tongue exactly twelve inches long! It was named **Xanthopan morgani praedicta** (the last part of the name because it had been formerly predicted).

1800s   **IN HAWAII** between 1810 and 1825, some people paid their taxes in coffee beans.

1800s   **IN VICTORIAN** times the poor were sometimes given a brew made from dried ash leaves with sheep's dung and passed off as tea.

FRUIT AND VEG

Here are some fruity (and veggie) facts to exchange with your greengrocer.

APPLES AND PEARS

THERE ARE over two thousand varieties of apple grown in Britain.

SOLD OUT

THE PHRASE 'An apple a day keeps the doctor away' was coined in 1904 by J.T. Stinson, Director of the Missouri State Fruit Experimental Station. He lived to be 92!

APPLES float because 25% of their volume is air.

THE PECTIN in apples may help digestive processes after a meal.

SUMMER PUD

STRAWBERRIES were the first frozen fruits to be sold in Britain.

IN ANGLO-SAXON, strawberries were called 'streabariye', as the strawberry plant puts out runners that allow it to stray from where it started.

STRAWBERRIES are the only fruit with the seeds on the outside. In fact, they are not strictly a fruit, botanically speaking, more of an enlarged receptacle covered in yellow pip-like fruits called achenes.

IT TAKES around ten kilos of cherries to make one litre of cherry liqueur.

TOTALLY TROPICAL

PINEAPPLES are made of several small fruits fused together.

A PINEAPPLE is ripe enough to eat when you can pull out one of its leaves with a sharp tug.

TRY THIS ONE!

IF YOU laid them end to end, the bananas picked in a year would go round the world two thousand times.

THERE IS NO such thing as a banana tree. They are herbaceous plants, i.e. without woody stems. Banana 'tree trunks' are made up of tightly overlapping leaves, similar to a leek. After fruiting the banana 'trees' are chopped back to be replaced by a new stem that grows up from the base.

SOME WILD bananas have large seeds, but commercially grown bananas are seedless and sterile. They have to be propagated vegetatively from side shoots.

A TROPICAL fruit called a durian smells like 'an open sewer', or 'a corpse'. Some say it tastes like vanilla custard and cream. Others liken its flavour to onion ice cream or ice cream that has been sieved through a sewer.

THE DURIAN is a favourite food of the orang-utan. The seeds pass through the gut unharmed and come out in the droppings some distance from the parent tree.

ORANGES AND LEMONS

LEMON TREES can produce lemons all year round and often have flowers and fruits on them at the same time.

AROUND 160,000 tonnes of oranges are harvested every day.

THERE IS a citrus fruit called the 'fingered citron' or 'Buddha's hand', that looks like a yellow rubber glove. In China it is used for perfuming rooms and clothes.

PEEL ME A GRAPE

JUICY FACTS!

TWENTY-TWO billion grapes are picked every day – that weighs in at roughly 155,000 tonnes.

STUFF YOU MAY NOT KNOW ABOUT POTATOES

POTATOES originated in the Andes in South America.

POTATOES have been part of our diet in Europe for around 400 years. They have been on the menu in South America for around 8,000 years. Pre-Inca civilizations (around 4,000 years ago) ate freeze-dried potatoes. They dug potatoes up and left them out overnight in the cold to freeze. They then thawed and squeezed them and refroze them the next night. This process was repeated for 3-4 nights. The result was the original freeze-dried potatoes.

SPUDS, YOU LIKE?

VEGGIES

PUMPKINS, marrows, courgettes and their relations are around 90% water.

GARLIC smells because of a sulphurous chemical in its bulb. Garlic-eaters smell because the body gets rid of some of the sulphur by turning it into methyl mercapan, which is then exhaled.

IF YOU really love garlic you can buy garlic ice cream and garlic beer from a specialist firm in London.

MOST of the garlic sold in Britain is grown on one farm on the Isle of Wight.

ONIONS have been grown and eaten in China and Japan since prehistoric times. This was the 'Welsh' or 'Japanese bunching' onion, a non-bulb form with hollow leaves.

IN 1578 the tomato was described as 'a strange plant and not found in this country, except in the gardens of some herbalists ... and is dangerous to be used.'

EDIBLE WOLF PEACH - that's how the Latin name for tomato, *Lycopersicon esculentum*, translates!

THE ITALIANS called tomatoes Pomme de Mori (Moorish apples). The French mistranslated this as Pommes d'amour (apples of love), so people decided they must be an aphrodisiac!

WHAT COLOUR are carrots? Originally they were white or purple. These were being grown on farms and in gardens in the thirteenth century. By the sixteenth century we were growing orange carrots, which are believed to have originated in Afghanistan.

THE LEEK is an emblem of Wales today, but the ancient Egyptians revered it as a sacred plant.

PRIZE LEEKS are hung upside-down at local shows to prevent people from pumping water into the leaves to plump them up for the big event.

SCARY STUFF

And you thought plants were pretty things that grow in gardens ...

STEALERS

THE RED threads of dodder (*Cuscuta epithymum*) scramble over gorse and heather and suck out its juices.

MISTLETOE, even though it has green leaves and can make its own food, stabs its suckers down into the sugar-carrying vessels of the apple tree.

BROOMRAPE, as its name suggests, takes its food from the roots of the broom plant.

RAFFLESIA, one of the smelliest plants in the world, gets its nutrients from the roots of a liana. The flower is the only bit you ever see, the rest of the plant lives underground.

STRANGLERS

STRANGLER FIGS don't fight their way up from the bottom, they start at the top. Seeds are dropped by birds high in the rainforest trees, and germinate and grow in the moisture in the branches. The shoots make for the light while the roots make for the ground. The roots start to take up water and nutrients, but is any credit given to the tree that got them started? Not likely! The strangler fig plant strangles it, taking its food, water, and eventually light. Finally the host tree expires, and the strangler fig remains hollow yet strong in its place.

THE COOL taste that we enjoy in mint is there to keep off would-be snackers (insects).

IF AN ANIMAL starts to chomp on an African acacia tree, the tree produces a warning gas which drifts to the other African acacia trees downwind. They then make a poison and protect themselves. So if you're mad enough to eat acacias, always remember to move upwind!

THE LATEX fluid produced by rubber trees and some other rainforest giants when cut is great for healing the cut. It is also possibly there to gum up insects' mouth parts before they can do too much damage!

YOU FIND insect-eating plants in soils that are poor in plant nutrients such as nitrates. They need to get their food from somewhere so they eat flies. Yum. Carnivorous plants are usually brightly coloured to attract their prey. In some plants, once trapped, the insects often drown in an acidic liquid and are then digested.

SOME BUG-EATING plants are deceptively pretty, not least in name, for example, the Australian pink petticoat plant.

CARNIVOROUS plants don't die if they don't get their 'meat' fix. They just stop growing.

KILLER PLANTS!
DANGER!

THE FACTS IN THIS SECTION REMIND US TO BE AS WARY OF MESSING WITH PLANTS AS WE WOULD BE OF PLAYING WITH SNAKES. SOME OF THEM ARE VERY POISONOUS INDEED. ALWAYS CHECK YOU KNOW WHAT YOU ARE EATING, AND ALWAYS WASH YOUR HANDS WHEN YOU COME IN FROM THE GARDEN.

POISONERS

IN THE 11th century the Scots killed invading Danes by adding henbane to their mead which killed them as they slept.

WHEN POTATOES and tomatoes were brought to Europe in the 16th century people were very suspicious of eating them at first. This was partly because they resembled the poisonous plants henbane and deadly nightshade a little too closely for comfort.

HENBANE (*Hyoscyamus niger*) contains the poisons hyoscyamine and scopolamine. In Homer's story the witch, Circe, turned Odysseus' shipmates into swine with a drink of henbane. One of the characteristics of the poisons in henbane is that they give victims the illusion of having turned into animals.

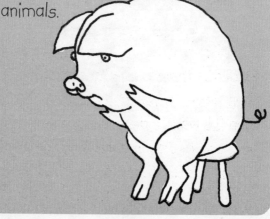

THE ANCIENT GAULS used henbane as a poison on their spears.

THE NOTORIOUS murderer Dr Crippen was hanged in 1910 for killing his wife with the poison hyoscine-hydrobromide, extracted from henbane.

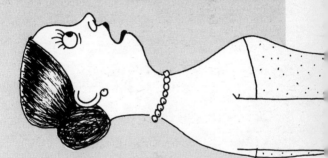

DEADLY NIGHTSHADE (*Atropa belladonna*) is also known as Belladonna (beautiful woman) after the ladies in ancient times who put drops of the juice, containing atropine, into their eyes to dilate their pupils and make themselves more attractive to men. It wasn't a good idea *because* deadly nightshade is very poisonous and can cause blindness, paralysis, coma and death.

THE ATROPA part of the Latin name for deadly nightshade (*Atropa belladonna*), is named after the Greek Fate Atropos, who cuts the threads of life. She was often portrayed holding deadly nightshade in her hand.

HEMLOCK (*Conium maculatum*) contains the poison coniine and was in the draught which killed Socrates in 399 BC. Onlookers were told that Socrates was becoming cold and numb from the feet up and that when the poison reached his heart he would die.

IT SEEMS to have been a pre-Christian custom to let hemlock grow outside the home to absorb any poison that might be about and keep the family healthy.

IN GREEK MYTH monkshood originated from the froth that dripped from the jaws of the three-headed dog Cerberus, when Hercules dragged him up from the underworld.

ACONITINE from monkshood may have led to the death of Emperor Claudius in AD 54. He was fed poisonous mushrooms, but they only made him sick. As was the custom, his throat was tickled with a feather to help him vomit, but the feather was spread with aconitine and succeeded in finishing him off.

ALL SORTS of myths surround the mandrake (*Mandragora officinarum*) because the root is shaped like a little human being. Pythagoras (born 582 BC) called the plant an anthropomorph (changes into a human).

IT WAS SAID that the mandrake uttered such a scream of terror when it was pulled up that those who heard it would die of fright.

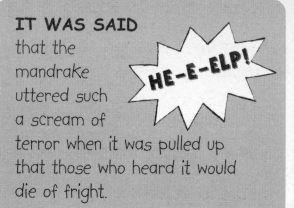

HE-E-ELP!

ORIGINATING in the eastern Mediterranean, the mandrake also contains the chemicals scopolamine and hyoscyamine. Ancient Persians and Egyptians used the yellow and red berries and the roots as aphrodisiacs.

THE MUSTARD plant contains chemical glycosides and an enzyme, which are kept quite separate. But the reaction between the two chemicals produces a powerful oily liquid. In the First World War vapour from the oil – mustard gas – was used as a biological weapon which caused horrendous burns and blindness.

TUMMY ACHES AND WORSE

GREEN POTATOES can make you ill because they contain the chemical solanine. Don't eat them.

SOME PLANTS contain phytophototoxins - substances that make non-pigmented or slightly pigmented skin hypersensitive to the ultraviolet radiation in sunlight. Rue and hogweed quite often cause skin blistering but some sensitive people get the same reaction from brushing against parsnip plants that have gone to seed. They cause the skin to redden and blister.

EATING RHUBARB can make your teeth feel hairy! This is due to the oxalic acid it contains (also in spinach). Rhubarb leaves contain much more of the chemical, so you shouldn't eat them. Eating rhubarb leaves makes people drowsy and sick and has even been fatal on some occasions.

NINE PIGS in America were poisoned after eating a wheelbarrowful of rhubarb leaves thrown to them as feed. They foamed at the mouth, staggered and died in convulsions three to four hours later.

THE LEAVES of stinging nettles are covered with stiff hairs full of poison (formic acid) which cause a painful rash called urticaria.

BEWARE OF THE PLANT

FRIENDLY old bracken is in fact the stuff of nightmares ... It's competitive and toxic. Its underground creeping stems grow at least a metre a year. The stem carries dormant fronds, which spring into life when the plant is cut.

SOME CACTI have spines up to 15 cm long – not bad for deterring grazing animals.

LOVE POTIONS AND BEAUTY

What better than fruit and flowers to soothe and smooth...

BEAUTY TIPS

PEOPLE used to rub strawberries on their teeth as a sort of early toothpaste. They were supposed to remove any discoloration and leave the teeth white. Or pink...

FRENCH society ladies used to redden their lips by biting into fresh lemons. They probably ended up with sour expressions!

LEMON essential oils are widely used by the toiletry industry in soaps, shampoo and toothpastes.

MASHED APPLES can be tried as a face pack. Apples are rich in fruit acids that can get rid of dead skin cells.

MASHED BANANA and grapeseed oil can be mixed together to make a conditioner for untangling frizzy hair. You might be better off buying one of the banana hair products on the market – probably less messy, and easier to wash out!

FOOD (AND DRINK) OF LOVE

THE POWDERED seed of coriander added to warm wine is supposed to make a lust potion.

CARRY BRAZIL nuts as a talisman for good luck in love affairs.

THE CHOCOLATE drink consumed by the Aztecs gained a reputation as a love potion because cocoa beans contain theobromine, a mild stimulant.

TO CAST a Japanese love spell, tie a strand of your hair to a blossoming wild cherry tree (*Prunus avium*).

FEED SWEET chestnuts to a sweetheart if you want your love to be reciprocated.

PAPAYA, if shared with a loved one, is said to intensify the feelings of love.

PLANTS USED by Druids in fertility magic included: bananas, birch, coconut, fig, mistletoe, oak, olive, orange, palm, pine, pomegranate, quince and willow. Some of these are poisonous. For love spells they used apple, apricot, avocado, brazil, cherry, sweet chestnut, lemon, papaya, plum, prickly ash, rose, walnut and willow.

THE WORD ORCHID derives from the word Greek word for testicle, due to the shape of the root. The dried tuberous roots of certain orchid species (of which there are over thirty thousand in all) have been used by herbalists in various cultures as an aphrodisiac.

AND THE ANTIDOTE

IF YOU are trying to rid yourself of a would-be wooer, pistachios are said to do the trick. The Arabs believed eating these was an antidote to love spells.

82

LOVES ME, LOVES ME NOT

ONE NORFOLK tradition said that if a man was after a particular girl he should take an orange, prick it all over with a pin in the pits of its skin and sleep with it under his armpit. The next day he was to give it to the girl - if she ate it in front of him then love was in the air.

TRY TO PEEL an apple in one long, unbroken strip. Then throw it over your left shoulder. It should fall in the shape of your loved one's initial.

IT'S THE LEAVES of a rose that are supposed to show you which admirer is true. Pick one leaf for each admirer and lay them out. The admirer whose leaf stays green the longest is the one for you.

A PARTNER'S faithfulness was also tested by putting named apple-pips on the edge of the fire and saying, 'If you love me, bounce and fly, and if you hate me, lie and die'.

WEDDING BOUQUETS

IN ANCIENT ROME a child would walk before the bride carrying a torch of whitethorn (*Sorbus aria*) in honour of Ceres. In the evening, hazel torches would be lit to ensure a peaceful and happy union.

THE RED ROSE is sacred to Venus, goddess of love, life, creation, fertility, beauty and virginity – and not necessarily in that order.

THE GREEKS decked their brides with hawthorn sprigs, and hawthorn boughs were also placed on the altar.

SARACEN BRIDES wore orange blossoms as a sign of fecundity (ability to have lots of children), a practice brought back to Europe by crusaders.

A WEDDING CUSTOM in parts of India is for the bride and groom to stand side by side in bamboo baskets. The groom then pours grains of rice over the bride's head.

POMEGRANATES were served at the marriage banquets of ancient Assyria and Babylonia as a symbol of love and plenty.

PIP PIP!

THE BIRDS, THE BEES...AND SEEDS

Some say plants can't move - so how do they get around ...?

SOWING WILD OATS

WILD OATS have two stiff hairs at the top of each seed, twisted like a coiled spring. When wet they uncoil and the seed crawls along the ground like a two-legged spider and drills its way down into suitable crevices in the soil.

LIKE WILD OATS, mangroves also plant their own seeds. They grow in tropical swamps. The seeds germinate while still attached to the plant and send down an exploratory root. When it is long enough, the plant lets go and the seed plops down into the mud.

GRAPE SEEDS are distributed by the creatures that eat the grapes – birds, foxes, bears, box turtles and primates.

DANDELIONS and groundsel have well-engineered parachute seeds, and sycamores have their own helicopters. Coltsfoot seeds have been found 14 km from their parents, and ragwort seeds over 100km.

GERONIMO!

BLACKBERRIES and many other fruits have their own airliners – birds. Seeds go in as a tasty snack and after the flight is over come out covered in ready-made fertilizer...

TAKING THIS PRINCIPLE one step further... The berries of the Australian mistletoe are very sticky. They pass through a bird's digestive system, but then stick to its backside, so the bird has to rub them off onto trees.

BLACKBERRY BRAMBLES 'flip' their way along. Their long, rapidly growing shoots turn earthwards, grow towards the ground, and develop roots. Then they send off another shoot, and so on. In New Zealand, they say there are only two blackberry plants; one on the North Island and one on the South Island.

TOMATO PLANTS are often found growing in sewage works – a perfect mode of transport, down the loo and off to a fertile seed bed.

CHICKWEED has a life cycle of only seven weeks but it can produce 15,000 million plants a year.

SOME ORCHIDS imitate both the smell and the appearance of bees and other insects to attract 'mates' who can help with pollination.

COME AND GET ME!

IVY-LEAVED toadflax grows on vertical walls. Its flowers face out to the sun, but once they are plump with seed they turn their heads back to the wall. When it rains, the seed spills into the wall ... ready for the next generation.

THERE IS an old wives' tale that recommends gardeners to sow seed during a waning rather than a waxing moon. There may be some truth in this, because the moon controls the tides, which in turn affect the Earth's atmosphere.

DURING PLANT pollination the grain of pollen grows a tail and swims, sperm-like, along the female tube (style) to the ovary, where it fertilizes the ovum.

STINKY AND SQUIRTY

STAPELIAS look like brown-and-yellow starfish, and they stink. The awful smell attracts flies, which pollinate the flower as they lay their eggs. When the eggs hatch, the maggots, being carnivores, die.

THE FRUIT of the squirting cucumber swells right up until it can't stay on the stem any longer, and then lets go. The juice and seeds squirt out through the hole left by the stem at around 100 km per hour. The same sort of idea is used to propel rocket engines in space vehicles.

CUCKOO PINT (*Arum maculatum*) has a hooded flower containing a purple, club-shaped organ called a spadix. This actually heats up when the flower opens, wafting the horrible smell to nearby flies. The flies head towards the basal chamber where downward-pointing hairs keep them there until they have pollinated the flower. The hairs then wilt and the flies escape.

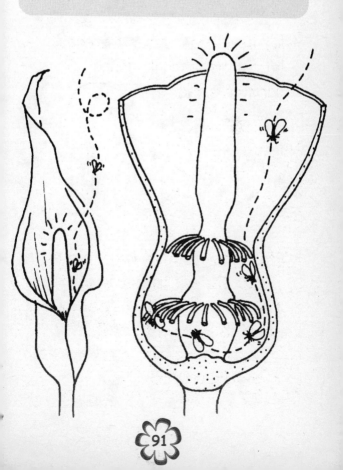

WHAT'S IN A NAME?

You can learn almost everything about a plant from its full botanical name, and quite a bit more from its traditional one. You can probably add some examples of your own.

DERIVATIONS

THE WORD 'orange' may come from the Arabic 'narandj' from the Sanskrit 'nagarunga' meaning 'fruit favoured by elephants'.

FRENCH for gooseberry is 'groseille'. 'Une femme grosse' is the term given to a pregnant woman in France. This may have led to the saying that babies come from under the 'gooseberry bush'.

THE WORD 'canvas' comes from the word 'cannabis', the Latin name for the industrial hemp from which canvas and other hemp fabrics are woven.

FUNKY FABRIC!

OUR WORD 'paper' comes from 'papyrus', a very tall type of grass with a chunky, triangular stem, which the Egyptians pressed into a writing material 6,000 years ago.

'RUBBER' is so-called simply because of its ability to rub out pencil marks.

PUMPKIN gets its name from the Greek 'pepon', meaning 'cooked by the sun'.

WHAT WE call a swede in Britain is actually a type of turnip. Swede is short for 'Swedish Turnip', as it was first imported from Sweden in the eighteenth century.

PUT-DOWNS

SEVENTEENTH-CENTURY alehouse owners losing custom to coffee-houses called coffee 'syrup and soot' and 'essence of old shoes'.

IN THE NINETEENTH century blackberries were known as 'bumblekites' and 'scaldheads' because children who ate too many were told they would get a disease in their hair.

MISNOMERS

THE GOLDEN APPLE of mythology was probably a lemon.

THE PROPER NAME for cocoa is cacao, but the Victorians couldn't pronounce it – hence cocoa.

WRONG!

NEW ANGLES

IN ITALY sweet oranges are known as blondes or blood.

WINE TASTERS can find tastes amongst wines such as: apples, earth, honey, blackcurrants, nuts, peaches, oak, flint, spice, smoke, truffles, stalks and violet.

IN MADAGASCAR people measure time according to how long it takes to cook a pot of rice (*indray mahamasa-bary*) rather than a certain number of minutes, and distance according to the time it takes to reach a destination. Thus they say that a place is located at a distance two or three times the time necessary to cook a pot of rice.

The East
The West
Next Services

FAMILY TREES

PLUMS are in the same family as roses.

CITRUS TREES (oranges, lemons etc.) are in the same family as the bitter-tasting herb, rue.

THE TOMATO PLANT is in fact a member of the potato family, and the tomato fruit is its large berry. Other members of the potato family with edible fruits include aubergines and cape gooseberries. Potatoes also produce tomato-like fruits but these are poisonous and cannot be eaten.

GREAT NAMES

EVERY CULTURE has its own pet names for plants. Usually the more common names a plant has the more useful it is or has been.

THE SHORTEST Latin name for a plant is *Aa*, and it belongs to an orchid from South America.

LATIN NAMES for plants are more fun than they first seem, as they are very descriptive. Here are some:

Coprosma – smelling of dung
Dysentericus – cures dysentery
Emeticus – causing vomiting
Foetidus – bad smelling
Furiens – exciting to madness
Gongylodes – swollen/roundish
Harrysmithii – In honour of Harry Smith, who collected it in China in the early 20th century
Hippobroma – drives horses mad
Hircinus – smelling of goat
Impudicus – lewd, shameless
Inflatus – inflated, swollen
Ingens – enormous
Onopordum – like an ass's fart

The stinkwood tree from New Zealand is called **Coprosma foetidissima**. Work that one out!

THIS IS HOW the botanical name for our 'daisy' breaks down:

Family: *Compositae* (means a flower made of many parts)
Genus: *Bellis* (means beautiful)
Species: *perennis* (means comes up every year)
Cultivar: 'Alba Plena', 'Alice', 'Annie', 'Dawn Raider' and so on.
Common name: Daisy (means 'day's eye' as daisies only open in the day)

THERE IS a story of a travelling botanist in the Amazon who found that many quite different-looking plants all had the same common name in the local language. When he enquired further he was told that the name meant 'completely useless'.

'WELCOME HOME, husband, though never so drunk' is an old name for stonecrop, the little succulent found growing on ancient walls - very convenient for unsteady drunks to grab hold of.

DANDELION, a mild diuretic, is called 'pisenlit' in France – or 'wet the bed'.

PILEWORT is a country name for lesser celandine, because the roots look like 'piles' (haemorrhoids) and were once used to treat them. This form of medicine was known as the 'doctrine of signatures'.

HERE'S A PLANT with a lot of names – the humble goosegrass. It is also known as cleavers, beggar weed, bleedy tongues, sticky willie and gentleman's tormentors. The seeds, called 'sweethearts', spread in pairs by sticking to passing animals.

YOU'LL HAVE TO guess the reason for the country name of the wild pansy (or heartsease) ... It's 'meet-her-in-the-entry-kiss-her-in-the-buttery'.

EXTREME PLANTS

All plants need air, water and sunshine to grow, but some manage to survive with very little of one or other of these conditions.

NO RAIN

THE RESURRECTION PLANT, *Selaginella lepidophylla,* dries out completely into a brown ball. When it gets water it immediately opens out and becomes green. The process is totally reversible.

NO WARMTH

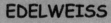

EDELWEISS has a furry flower that acts like a fur coat to keep the plant warm, and prevent water loss.

THE ALPINE snowbell has a tiny shoot that produces enough heat to melt a hole in the snow for it to reach the surface and flower in early spring.

LIFE AT 83°C (AND FREEZING AT NIGHT)

FENESTRARIA lives in the desert buried in the sand to protect itself from animals and the searing heat. Only the tips of the leaves show – these are transparent and act like magnifying glasses to catch the sun. It gets its name from the Latin word for window – fenestra.

OCOTILLO (*Fouquieria splendens*) plants survive drought by dropping all their leaves, growing a new set only when it rains.

SOME DESERT PLANTS have woolly coats to insulate the plant from the heat and the cold.

CACTUS SPINES deter would-be predators. They also lose less water than leaves would because they have less surface area.

WHEN PLANTS photosynthesize in the day they open their leaf pores (stomata) to get the carbon dioxide (CO_2) they need to make sugar. If cacti did this they would lose lots of water out of the holes through evaporation in the sun, so they photosynthesize at night instead. To get round the fact there is no sun at night, they do the bit that needs sun in the day and make a halfway house food – special acids. They complete the rest of the process at night using CO_2 to turn the acid to sugar. The acidity in cactus sap therefore changes about 4000% between night and day.

THE SEEDS of many desert plants lie dormant in the soil awaiting a shower. *Boerhavia repens* seeds germinate as soon as it rains, then grow, flower, seed and die in just ten days.

CREOSOTE BUSHES preserve space around themselves because their roots give off a poison to stop other plants from growing too close.

MASOCHISTIC PLANTS

SOME ALGAE can grow in water that is near boiling point.

DANDELION and dock roots don't mind being chopped up and docks even survive torture. A dock plant was once dug up and nailed to a shed wall for two years. On replanting, it grew. Dock roots contain their own natural 'antibacterial potion' so they don't rot very easily, even on the compost heap.

BULLY BOYS

JAPANESE Knotweed is an aggressive weed that was introduced into Britain in 1825. By 1879 it was described as 'a plant of sterling merit, now becoming quite common'. Today, in Britain, it is illegal to propagate or deliberately plant it in a garden. It is a very troublesome weed and almost impossible to eradicate. The underground stems, or rhizomes, are sometimes so thick that a saw is needed to cut them.

PLANT DOCTOR

Until recently people nearly always sought remedies for illness from the plants around them. Many modern medicines are still based on plants.

HEALTHY FRUIT

YOU OFTEN see tennis players eating bananas during a match. Wimbledon competitors have been known to get through eight hundred a day between them! Bananas provide slow-release energy and contain potassium, which may help to prevent cramp.

RASPBERRIES are rich in vitamins and minerals and have been said to help cure diseased gums, upset stomachs and even diarrhoea.

GRAPES are good for you. In the eighteenth and nineteenth centuries cures using grapes were known as ampelotherapy.

SOME PEOPLE recommend chewing grapes to cure infected gums. Others say that a grape diet will help a whole range of ailments, including skin problems.

LIMES were used by British sailors (dubbed limeys) to provide vitamin C to help prevent scurvy on long sea voyages. Limes contain around 46mg of vitamin C per 100g.

ANCIENT HERBALISTS used blackberries and their juices to treat eye and mouth infections. This would really give you a black eye – and a black mouth!

IN HAWAII pineapples are taken as a cure for indigestion. Pineapple has been found to contain an enzyme, bromelain, that breaks down dead tissue containing proteins and so helps to digest meat.

EAT YOUR VEG

LEEKS are renowned for their medicinal value and internal cleansing powers and have been cultivated in the west for up to four thousand years.

ASPARAGUS is sometimes recommended for people who suffer from arthritis and rheumatism.

BEETROOT helps to cleanse the blood and is still used in Russia to help people build up resistance to disease.

GLOBE artichokes are reputedly good for the heart and have been used in European folk medicine to ward off heart attacks.

GARLIC, King cure, has been used to treat heart problems, cancer, bronchitis – and even old age in some places!

BROCCOLI is supposed to give protection against some forms of cancer.

PEOPLE used to drink raw cabbage juice as a treatment for ulcers.

THE CUP THAT CHEERS

COFFEE is a strong stimulant. One cup of strong-brewed, freshly ground coffee contains around 150mg caffeine, enough to stimulate the nervous system. Larger doses can impair performance, especially where delicate co-ordination is required. Several strong cups a day can cause anxiety and restlessness.

IN JAPAN green-tea-stuffed armrests are on sale. The tea fragrance is said to relax the mind.

SCIENTISTS at the National Cancer Institute in America have recommended tea as the most suitable drink for astronauts on the proposed eight-year mission to Mars, because tea may help to neutralize the harmful effects of radiation encountered in space.

ANCIENT AND MODERN LORE

ARISTOTLE remarked that elephants could be cured of insomnia by rubbing a concoction of salt, olive oil and water into their shoulders!

AN IMPORTANT health manual written in Roman times was *De Materia Medica* by Dioscorides (AD 40-90). Dioscorides, an army doctor from Asia Minor, described the medicinal use of over 600 plants, including belladonna, calamine and opium.

ONE OF the most famous instances of a wild flower being the basis of a modern drug is the foxglove (*Digitalis purpurea*). In the eighteenth century country people were known to use it to cure dropsy – a condition where patients became bloated. The side effect was a speeding up of the heartbeat. Now a drug made from foxglove is used to regulate the heart.

CHEMICALS contained in the pretty Madagascar periwinkle, *Catharanthus roseus*, have provided a major breakthrough in the treatment of childhood leukaemia.

THE CHEMICAL from a vine used by Amazonian people to paralyse animals is used by hospital anaesthetists as a muscle-relaxant for their patients.

FOR CENTURIES people treated aches and pains with willow (*Salix*), using both the bark and the leaves. The wildflower meadowsweet was also used. The common ingredient was salicin, which we find today in aspirin.

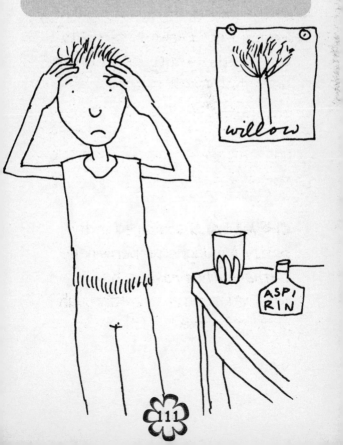

willow

ASPI RIN

QUININE, used to treat malaria since the seventeenth century, originally came from the bark of the South American tree, *Cinchona succirubra*. Quinine is now manufactured artificially.

TONIC WATER is made with quinine. Many people developed a taste for it when dosing themselves daily against malaria, hence the penchant for gin and tonic amongst the Europeans living in India when it was part of the British Empire.

CRUCIAL CROPS

There are around 250,000 plant species in the world. Five – maize, rice, wheat, potato and cassava – feed most of the world's people.

RICE

IMPORTANT!

RICE IS the world's largest crop and feeds half the world's population.

RICE IS farmed on every continent except for Antarctica.

THERE ARE over seventy thousand varieties of rice.

HEMP

GEORGE WASHINGTON said, 'Make use of hemp seed, sow it everywhere.'

THE ORIGINAL Levi's were made from hemp.

'OVER 25,000 products can be manufactured from hemp, from cellophane to dynamite'. *Popular Mechanics Magazine*, 1938.

TODAY Ford are experimenting with the use of hemp bio-composites in car body parts. In  the 1940s Ford had a vision of 'growing automobiles from the soil' and even produced a demonstration model with body parts partially made of hemp.

NAPOLEON'S war with Russia was due partially to a hemp supply shortage.

COTTON

AS WELL as being spun into yarn for cloth, cotton is also often used in tooth-paste, explosives, ice cream, sausage skins, paint, wallpaper, and even edible oils.

TEA

TEA is intricately linked with Western cultural history. The incident popularly believed to have triggered the American Revolution was the 'Boston Tea Party' in December 1773, when Bostonians dressed as Indians protested against the tax on tea and the monopoly of the East India Company. They boarded three tea ships in the harbour by moonlight and tipped the tea chests overboard.

RUBBER

RUBBER, once used for waterproofing coats and erasing pencil marks, now helps to transport us across the world in the form of cars and aircraft. In some parts of the United States, tyre rubber has been recycled as a hardwearing road surface.

OLIVES

OLIVE OIL is becoming the superfood of the 21st century because it contains antioxidants which keep 'free radicals' in food at bay. 'Free radicals', made when polyunsaturated fats in the body combine with oxygen, can damage cell membranes and even break down DNA.

FANTASTIC PLASTIC

THE PLASTICS industry is starting to make plastic from plants as well as from fossil fuels. Maize is the main material at present, but potatoes and wheat are following close behind. As well as being biodegradable, plant plastics can be composted to make a natural fertilizer.

YOU WILL already find plastics made from the starch in maize in plastic cutlery, packaging, disposable nappies, pens, toys and many other items.

A TRANSPARENT plastic made using corn syrup (also from maize) is found in food containers, films, sweet wrappers, envelope windows, and yoghurt pots.

SOYBEANS can be made into a biodegradable soy-based plastic that breaks down in only 10-14 days.

117

FANCY THAT!

Try these ones out on your friends!

THERE ARE about 250,000 plant species in the world. Plants are the dominant life form on planet Earth, making up over 99% of the biomass.

MAHATMA GANDHI drank grape juice to keep him going during his marathon fasts.

BOTANISTS have been known to dangle from hovering helicopters to pluck seeds from the tops of palms.

THE MAYA people of ancient Mesoamerica used the valuable cocoa bean as currency.

IN CENTRAL AMERICA chocolate is traditionally served as a bitter breakfast drink - sometimes with chillies (hot hot chocolate!).

IN BURMA and Bangladesh half the houses are made almost entirely from bamboo.

BAMBOO, dubbed the plant of 1001 uses, can be made into many things from bridges to bicycles, gramophone needles to scaffolding.

THE I CHING (Book of Changes), one of the oldest books in the world, is written on bamboo tablets.

HAVE YOU EVER seen a square bamboo pole? In Japan they grow square bamboo poles by placing a square wooden mould over the shoots as they grow.

THE COMPOSER Beethoven was said to use 60 beans for every cup of coffee he consumed.

SCIENTISTS in the US tried out drugs on spiders to see what happened to their webs. Caffeine, found in coffee and tea, disrupted their weaving more severely than marijuana.

TREES carry on growing all their lives.

ONE 'DIESEL' TREE (*Copaiba – Copaifera multijuga*) from the Amazon can yield 220 litres of a diesel-like oil a day, enough to fill up five cars.

THE EARLIEST OLYMPIC flame was probably a burning olive bough.

IN CHINA some people eat roast hemp seeds rather than popcorn at the cinema.

OUR OXYGEN comes from plants. 70% of the planet's oxygen comes from the sea, made by trillions of algae that float around in the waves.

THE BIG O

ENOUGH COTTON is harvested around the world EVERY DAY to make 500 million pairs of underpants.

A SINGLE grass plant can cover a whole field.

UNDER every square metre of garden lawn, there are around thirty thousand seeds.

WE EVOLVED to live on the waste products of plants. (Oxygen – think about it!)

THOUGHT FOR THE DAY

PEAS AND BEANS can make fertilizer out of fresh air. They work in partnership with bacteria called rhizobia that live in the plant roots. The bacteria get a free home and a supply of sugar that is made by the plant. They pay their rent by turning the nitrogen in the air into nitrogen-rich plant food for their landlord, the plant.

SOME FLOWERS are 'bee purple'. Evening primroses look yellow to us but purple to bees. Many flowers, such as geraniums, have landing strips on their leaves that only bees can see.

THE VENUS FLYTRAP with its jaws of death is a plant that can count ...

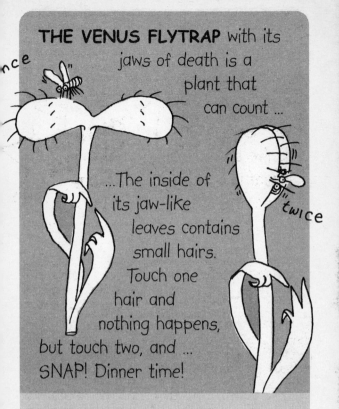

...The inside of its jaw-like leaves contains small hairs. Touch one hair and nothing happens, but touch two, and ... SNAP! Dinner time!

THE HOOKED SEEDS

of burdock were the inspiration behind the fastening material Velcro, invented by Swiss designer George de Mestral.

LIANAS, the Tarzan jungle vines, use the trees to support them. They can grow up to 300 metres, taller than Canary Wharf, and are strong enough to take the weight of a small truck.

123

A BIRD IN THE BUSH

In 1957, 83-year-old Mrs Louisa Bird became so entangled in a blackberry bush by a railway path that she was unable to escape. She was trapped for a whole cold night, and was only spotted by chance when a resident opened her curtains the next morning and saw the bush shaking. It took three policemen and a passer-by to free her using wire cutters. Mrs Bird kept her strength up during the ordeal by eating all the blackberries within reach.

SUNFLOWER SEEDS were used by the Hopi Indians as a source of dye for body paint and in pottery – long before anyone invented sunflower margarine.

APPARENTLY, THE RAREST and most valuable botanical jewel is a pearl found in a coconut (*Cocos nucifera*). The chances of finding one of these inside a coconut are less than one in a million. Strangely, botanists can't agree on whether such a pearl really exists, but the famous Maharajah coconut pearl is on display at the Fairchild Tropical Gardens in Florida.

WE ALL KNOW the rainforest is disappearing fast. For the record, while you are reading this paragraph we will probably have lost an area of forest the size of the Eden Project in Cornwall (around 100 acres a minute).

STOP!

POPPY SEEDS can remain dormant for over 100 years. They spring into life when they get a flash of sunlight. In World War One poppies grew next to the trenches when the soil was exposed to light but they came to symbolize the blood of the soldiers who died there.

THE BULL'S HORN ACACIA has barracks in its thorns that contain armies of ants. They get free food and housing in return for patrolling the tree and chucking out would-be predators.

IN THE 1880s Engelmann, a German botanist, discovered that it is the red and blue parts of sunlight that are converted into food energy. The leaves of plants look green because they absorb red and blue light but reflect the green (which they don't use).

VALENTINE SALAD: Lettuce be married. I'll beetroot to you to the endive my days.

QUIZ
ANSWERS

1. rubber

2. coconut

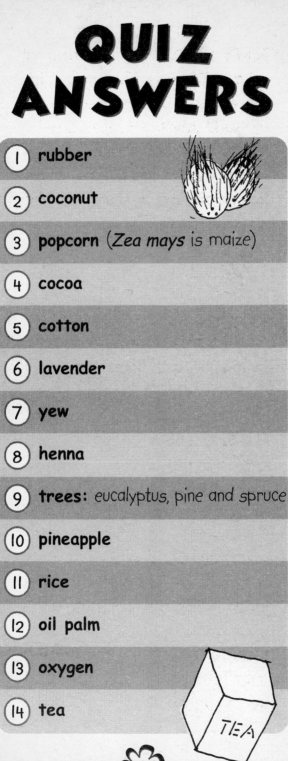

3. popcorn (*Zea mays* is maize)

4. cocoa

5. cotton

6. lavender

7. yew

8. henna

9. **trees:** eucalyptus, pine and spruce

10. pineapple

11. rice

12. oil palm

13. oxygen

14. tea

TEA